W9-CBL-302

ALBERT'S
Impossible
Toothache

Barbara Williams

illustrated by Doug Cushman

CANDLEWICK PRESS
CAMBRIDGE, MASSACHUSETTS

One morning Albert Turtle
complained that he had a toothache.

"Whoever heard of a turtle with a toothache?" said Albert's sister, Marybelle.

Just the same, Albert was sure he had a toothache and needed to stay in bed.

"See," said Albert's father, pointing to his own toothless mouth. "I don't have a toothache. And Homer doesn't have a toothache. And Marybelle doesn't have a toothache. And your mother doesn't have a toothache. It's impossible for anyone in our family to have a toothache."

"You never believe me," said Albert.

"I'd believe you if you told the truth," said Albert's father.

"You believed Homer when he said he didn't break the window," Albert reminded his father.

"I'm worried about Albert," said Albert's mother at breakfast.

"You *should* be worried about a boy who doesn't tell the truth," said Albert's father as he left for work.

"Albert just doesn't want to eat his black ants," said Marybelle.

"If I had a toothache, I'd still want to eat my black ants," announced Homer.

"Come eat your black ants, Albert," called his mother.

But Albert just moaned softly from the bedroom.

Albert's mother kissed Homer and Marybelle
goodbye and sat down in her worrying chair.

She worried and worried.

Then she had an idea.

"Look," she said to Albert. "I've fixed you a special breakfast of all your favorite things — dandelion leaves garnished with blackberries, a fat slug, and half a juicy earthworm."

"I can't eat anything," said Albert. "I have a toothache."

"Of course you don't have a toothache," said his mother.

"You never believe me," said Albert.

"I'd believe you if you told the truth," said Albert's mother.

"You believed Dad when he said he caught a seven-pound trout," Albert reminded her.

Albert's mother took the tray back to the kitchen and
went outside to her worrying swing on the porch.
She worried and worried.

Then she had another idea.

"Come play catch with me," she said. "You can teach me how to throw a knuckle ball."

"I can't teach you how to throw a knuckle ball," said Albert. "I have a toothache."

"You just think you have a toothache," said Albert's mother.

"You never believe me," whined Albert. "You believed Marybelle when she said she was the only girl in her class who couldn't go to a birthday sleepover on a school night."

Albert's mother put the ball and glove away and
went outside to her worrying rock in the sun.
She worried and worried.

Then she had a new idea.

"Look, Albert, I brought the family album to show you the pictures we took in Disneyland. Sit up, Albert."

"I can't sit up," said Albert. "Why don't you ever believe me?"

Albert's mother put the family album away and went into the living room to lie down on her worrying sofa.

She worried and worried.

She was still worrying when Marybelle and Homer came home.

"How's Albert?" asked Marybelle.

"He still says he has a toothache," said Albert's mother.

"He just didn't want to fight Dilworth Dunlap," explained Marybelle. "He was waiting for Albert after school."

"If I had a toothache, I'd still fight Dilworth Dunlap," announced Homer.

"Is that son of ours still playing possum?" Albert's father asked when he got home from work.

"Yes," said Albert's mother. "I wish that he would remember he's a turtle."

"He just knew we were having cricket legs for dinner," said Marybelle.

"I don't want any cricket legs either," said Homer.

After dinner Grandmother Turtle came over with gummy worms for all the children.

"Can I have Albert's?" asked Marybelle. "He won't want it. He says he has a toothache."

"Isn't that terrible?" said Albert's mother.

"Can you believe your grandson would say an impossible thing like that?" asked Albert's father.

"The trouble with all of you is that you never believe him," said Albert's grandmother.

Albert's grandmother went into his bedroom.
"Well," she said. "I hear you have a toothache."
"Yes'm," said Albert.
"*Where* do you have a toothache?" asked Albert's grandmother.

"On my left toe," said Albert. "A gopher bit me when I stepped in his hole."

"Well, I have just the thing to fix a toothache," said Albert's grandmother. She took her handkerchief from her purse and wrapped it around Albert's toe.

Albert smiled toothlessly and got out of bed.

For Kim
B. W.

To my expat writing friends and dinner companions in Paris —
Liberté, Egalité, Fromager!
D. C.

First Candlewick Press edition 2003

Library of Congress Cataloging-in-Publication Data

Williams, Barbara.
Albert's impossible toothache / Barbara Williams ;
illustrated by Doug Cushman. —1st Candlewick Press ed.
p.   cm.
Summary: When Albert complains of a toothache, no one in his family
believes him, until his grandmother takes the time to really listen to him.
ISBN 0-7636-1723-7
[1. Turtles—Fiction. 2. Family life—Fiction.
3. Listening—Fiction.] I. Cushman, Doug, ill. II. Title.
PZ7.W65587 Al 2003
[E]—dc21   2002067059

2 4 6 8 10 9 7 5 3 1

Printed in Italy

This book was typeset in Horley.
The illustrations were done in ink, watercolor, and colored pencil.

Candlewick Press
2067 Massachusetts Avenue
Cambridge, Massachusetts 02140

visit us at www.candlewick.com